THE MOONLIGHT ROOM

BY TRISTINE SKYLER

★

★

DRAMATISTS
PLAY SERVICE
INC.

THE MOONLIGHT ROOM

SPECIAL NOTE

Anyone receiving permission to produce THE MOONLIGHT ROOM is required to give credit to the Author as sole and exclusive Author of the Play on the title page of all programs distributed in connection with performances of the Play and in all instances in which the title of the Play appears for purposes of advertising, publicizing or otherwise exploiting the Play and/or a production thereof. The name of the Author must appear on a separate line, in which no other name appears, immediately beneath the title and in size of type equal to 50% of the size of the largest, most prominent letter used for the title of the Play. No person, firm or entity may receive credit larger or more prominent than that accorded the Author. The following acknowledgments must appear on the title page in all programs distributed in connection with performances of the Play:

Produced Off-Broadway by Arielle Tepper and Freddy DeMann.

Originally presented by The Worth Street Theatre Company and Solecist Prdns.

ACKNOWLEDGMENTS

Thank you to Brendan Sexton III, The Group at Strasberg, The Worth Street Theatre Company, James Adams, Craig Cohen, Ben and Annabelle Bierbaum, Matt Brown, Michael DeLuca, Michael Cardonick, and my family for invaluable help.

AUTHOR'S NOTE

Since the play takes place in a waiting room of a hospital, it is important to consider that the real "action" of the play takes place offstage. The circumstances are ever-present, and yet speak for themselves. Though a waiting room is a place to wait and reflect, hopefully the stage directions are useful to keep the pace of the play.

THE MOONLIGHT ROOM was originally produced by the Worth Street Theatre Company (Carol R. Fineman and Vern T. Calhoun, Producers) in association with Solecist Prdns at the Tribeca Playhouse in New York City. This production was subsequently produced Off-Broadway by Arielle Tepper and Freddy DeMann at the Samuel Beckett Theatre, opening on March 1, 2004. It was directed by Jeff Cohen; the set design was by Marion Williams; the lighting design was by Scott Bolman; the sound design was by Laura Grace Brown; the costume design was by Kim Gill; and the production stage manager was Michal V. Mendelson. The cast was as follows:

SAL .... Laura Breckenridge
MR. WELLS .... Lawrence James
MRS. KELLY .... Kathryn Layng
ADAM .... Mark Rosenthal
JOSHUA .... Brendan Sexton III

CHARACTERS

SAL, a girl, sixteen years old. Shy, vulnerable.

JOSHUA, a boy, sixteen years old. Smart, restless, someone who is always trying to rise above the turmoil he feels.

MRS. KELLY, a woman in her early forties, Sal's mother. Divorced, lonely, trying her best.

MR. WELLS, an African-American man in his late forties. Brave, stoic, dignified.

ADAM, a doctor in his late twenties. Extremely bright, but awkward, his confidence lies only in his knowledge.

PLACE

The action takes place in the waiting area of the emergency room of a hospital, on the Upper East Side of Manhattan, in New York City.

An interior set of an emergency room waiting area, which should include a pay phone, a vending machine, and an entrance/exit leading to the nurse's station and the rest of the hospital. There should be at least one row of three or more chairs, possibly more. They should be situated possibly at an angle, and/or more to one side of the stage than the center. The set should only suggest a portion of a waiting room, and not the whole room.

TIME

The present.

THE MOONLIGHT ROOM

ACT ONE

Scene 1

In the darkness the abrupt, piercing sound of a pager going off. As if an alarm. Lights up on a waiting room. Light gray walls, drab institutional furnishings. We see a row of orange chairs, the type that are each connected to another. On the wall to the right is a pay phone. The entrance/exit to the hospital is off to stage right. The hallway to the nurse's station is off to stage left. On the far upstage left are a couple of vending machines. The waiting area is deserted. A sixteen-year-old girl sits in the waiting area. She wears jeans or corduroys that hang down low, and an old T-shirt, as well as some jewelry and makeup. Her down jacket hangs over the seat next to her. She sits in silence for a few beats. She adjusts herself restlessly, looks at her surroundings. She waits. A thin boy (Joshua) about her age walks into the waiting room. He is dressed about the same as she is, just more so. He is wearing a hooded sweatshirt and no jacket. He looks at her nonchalantly. He takes his pager out of his pocket and looks at it. He goes to the phone booth and begins to dial, and then looks at the number on his pager, and then at the number on the pay phone. He hangs up the phone.

JOSHUA. *(Annoyed.)* I was paged to *this* pay phone.
SAL. I didn't know where you went.
JOSHUA. *(Simply.)* I went to get cigarettes. *(Sal doesn't respond. Josh sits down, a couple of seats away, and then stands up restlessly.)* It's

dropped ten degrees since we got here … At least ten. Maybe more. *(He pauses.)* I'm also sensing a rise in the barometric pressure …

SAL. *(Cutting him off, not angry, just concerned.)* Where'd you go?!

JOSHUA. The pressure of the air against the earth …

SAL. Josh!

JOSHUA. The deli on the corner was closed! I had to walk to Second Avenue.

SAL. You were gone a long time.

JOSHUA. Then the fucking Korean carded me. So I had to get Tirese to buy them for me.

SAL. Who's Tirese?

JOSHUA. This homeless guy who was selling key chains with miniature golf balls attached to them.

SAL. Did you buy one?

JOSHUA. *(Sarcastically.)* I didn't know it was your birthday.

SAL. *(Defensively.)* He bought you a pack of cigarettes!

JOSHUA. He bought himself one too.

SAL. Oh. *(He opens up his pack of cigarettes and is about to light one up.)*

JOSHUA. Do you think … *(He stops and glances around.)* Forget it.

SAL. What?

JOSHUA. Do you think we can smoke in here?

SAL. I doubt it.

JOSHUA. Why not?

SAL. What do you think?

JOSHUA. I don't know.

SAL. *(Simply.)* It's a hospital.

JOSHUA. Right. *(There is silence for a few beats. He considers his options.)* How about a beer?

SAL. You bought beer too?!

JOSHUA. I thought you had some in the car?

SAL. It's my mom's.

JOSHUA. Why does your mom keep the trunk of her car stocked with beer?

SAL. She went to the Price Club today.

JOSHUA. She hasn't unloaded the car?

SAL. You said we were in a rush to get there tonight before the line!

JOSHUA. That's true. *(Pause.)* I think … I think your mom will understand.

SAL. No, she won't.

JOSHUA. Yes, she will.

SAL. No, she won't!
JOSHUA. I'll replace the fucking beer!
SAL. Fine! *(She throws her car keys at him. He catches them and walks offstage right with his backpack. Sal sits motionless for a moment. She reaches in her pocket and counts her change. She has only a few dollars. She looks at her watch. Joshua enters. He sits down. He pulls a Budweiser from a six-pack that he now has hidden in his backpack.)*
JOSHUA. Did you know that Budweiser has formaldehyde in it?
SAL. Shut up.
JOSHUA. I'm serious. It's a preservative.
SAL. That's ridiculous.
JOSHUA. How else can it sit in your mom's car for a few months?
SAL. Very funny.
JOSHUA. Or better yet, so it can sit on the shelf at the Price Club — the white trash warehouse for bulk quantity discount.
SAL. You've never been there.
JOSHUA. Yes I have!
SAL. You have to be a member.
JOSHUA. My aunt is a member.
SAL. That's nice.
JOSHUA. And she's also overweight.
SAL. Is there a correlation?
JOSHUA. Of course. Everything they sell is oversized. It's proportionate. *(He laughs. Sal perhaps not willingly.)* Next to my aunt, a two foot tall jar of spaghetti sauce looks normal. *(Joshua looks to his right and then to his left to make sure no one can see him, and then he opens the can of beer. He looks at it suspiciously. He takes a sip.)* It's skunked!
SAL. She just got it!
JOSHUA. Well it's been sitting in your car rotting!
SAL. I thought you just said it had formaldehyde in it!
JOSHUA. No it doesn't!
SAL. That's what you said.
JOSHUA. What are you talking about? *(He gets up and empties the beer in the trash can and tosses the can.)*
SAL. That's what you said. A second ago. That's what you said. *(Josh doesn't answer.)* You always contradict yourself. You say something and then five minutes later you deny it.
JOSHUA. I have no short-term memory.
SAL. That's not true.
JOSHUA. What did I just say?

SAL. Lightfield rattled off the directions to the club and you remembered them. You didn't even write them down.
JOSHUA. I've been there before.
SAL. You said you hadn't!
JOSHUA. I didn't know until we walked in. *(Sal shakes her head in disgust. There is an awkward silence.)* Next to my aunt, a box of Special K that is three feet tall …
SAL. *(Cutting him off.)* They use that stuff to tranquilize horses.
JOSHUA. No they don't.
SAL. Yes they do.
JOSHUA. No they don't. *(Slowly, authoritatively.)* They use it on *dogs.*
SAL. Horses.
JOSHUA. Dogs!
SAL. *Horses!*
JOSHUA. You know how big horses are? If he was on horse tranquilizers right now he'd be in a fucking coma! *(There is another silence. Over the loudspeaker a page for a doctor is heard. Sal nervously looks at her watch.)* You know that kid Sajit? He had to go to the hospital and have his stomach pumped, and he was fine after.
SAL. *(Skeptically.)* Fine?
JOSHUA. *(Cheerfully.)* He went back to the party!
SAL. *(Not buying it.)* No, he didn't!
JOSHUA. Yes he did. But he smoked pot. He didn't drink. *(There is a pause. Joshua gestures to the rest of the six-pack in his backpack.)* Should I go put this back in the trunk?
SAL. Yes, and leave her stuff alone. *(He exits. Sal looks to stage left in the direction of the nurse's station. She seems unsure of what to do. She looks at her watch again. Joshua returns with an oversized jar of peanut butter.)* Josh!
JOSHUA. Aren't you hungry?
SAL. You're really pissing me off. If my mom is up, she's going to start freaking out. *(Josh starts eating the peanut butter.)*
JOSHUA. What time are you supposed to be back?
SAL. Three.
JOSHUA. That's ridiculous.
SAL. Why is it ridiculous? It's a good curfew.
JOSHUA. What's the point? You might as well stay out all night.
SAL. *(Condescendingly.)* The point is, that it allows her to know whether she needs to worry or not. If it's after three and I'm not there, then she knows it's okay to worry. It's a marker.

JOSHUA. That's a healthy way to go through life. Schedule your tension in advance. *(Sal doesn't answer.)* Your mom sounds interesting. *(Sal still doesn't answer.)* I'm not the type of person you have to worry about. My mom saw my potential early on.
SAL. Oh really?
JOSHUA. One day when I was seven she took me to John Jay. She didn't take me to the park that much because she didn't have the time. But this was a Saturday. I was at the swings. I had this pair of binoculars that I had sent away for from the back of *Sub-Mariner*. They'd just come in the mail that day and this kid said he'd hold them while I went on the swings. But when I got off he wouldn't give them back. And he had a knife, right? In a second I drop-kicked him and had them out of his hands. My mom witnessed the whole incident.
SAL. What did she do?
JOSHUA. Nothing. She didn't have to.
SAL. Good then can you get us out of this mess too?
JOSHUA. You're being dramatic again. *(Casually.)* He's going to be fine. *(There is a pause.)*
SAL. We went to that park. Carl Schurtz was better. But we stopped going when my mom got the car.
JOSHUA. Do you know that you and your mother manage to have a completely suburban lifestyle right in the middle of New York City.
SAL. That's not true.
JOSHUA. Yes it is. I was thinking about it when I went out to the car. Case in point. The fact that you have a car! And you are certainly the only people who drive to New Jersey to go to the Price Club.
SAL. *(Angry.)* Cut it out! She's going to start making calls pretty soon.
JOSHUA. No, she won't.
SAL. Yes she will. She'll call Lightfield's dad.
JOSHUA. *(Defensively.)* So what?
SAL. She'll say that we were with you.
JOSHUA. So?
SAL. He doesn't like you.
JOSHUA. He loves me.
SAL. What about his birthday party?
JOSHUA. That was nothing! When Lightfield was shooting that movie, I was the only one of his friends that was allowed to visit. I kept his dad company while he was working. They have something called craft services. It's all the food you could ever want. Sandwiches, fruit, Doritos …

SAL. *That's* where you got the name?
JOSHUA. Yeah.
SAL. Jesus.
JOSHUA. Can you think of a better name?
SAL. For selling pot? No, actually.
JOSHUA. *(Correcting her.) Delivering.* There's a difference.
SAL. *(Sarcastically.)* Excuse me.
JOSHUA. *(He's been through this a million times.)* I worked for the dealer. *He* developed and marketed the product, I just delivered it.
SAL. Josh …
JOSHUA. You don't call the paper boy the editor-in-chief?
SAL. We don't have paper boys in the city.
JOSHUA. No, we don't. But you and your mom probably do.
SAL. *(Sarcastic.)* Funny.
JOSHUA. Besides, marijuana is not a drug. It's a *pastime.* There's a difference.
SAL. No. *Golf* is a pastime. Marijuana is a drug.
JOSHUA. What are you talking about? You can't compare golf to marijuana.
SAL. I'm not.
JOSHUA. Yes you are! You said, "Golf is a pastime. Marijuana is a drug." You made a comparison.
SAL. No, making a comparison would be to find a way in which they were A) similar or B) different.
JOSHUA. What is this, English class? *(Facetiously.)* Is this a metaphor or a simile?
SAL. It's neither.
JOSHUA. Besides, golf isn't a pastime. *Stamp collecting* is a pastime. Golf is a sport.
SAL. Alright, enough!
JOSHUA. You're the one who made the comparison.
SAL. I wasn't comparing them.
JOSHUA. My dad plays golf.
SAL. *(Finally reaching her limit.)* Would you just please go find out what's going on?! *(Josh looks at his watch. He stands up.)*
JOSHUA. Fine.
SAL. Didn't they say they would come out and talk to us?
JOSHUA. These things don't need to be dragged out unnecessarily. *(Joshua is about to head to the nurse's station. Sal reaches her arm out to stop him.)*
SAL. Josh?

JOSHUA. What?
SAL. *(Thinks better of it.)* Forget it. *(Joshua exits, leaving the peanut butter on the seat. Sal picks it up and smells it. But she can't work up an appetite so she puts it back down. She waits. For a while. She takes out a pocket mirror from her backpack and a lipstick and puts it on. Josh returns.)*
JOSHUA. *(Casually.)* Should be any minute now.
SAL. What did she say?
JOSHUA. It won't be much longer.
SAL. Did the nurse say anything?
JOSHUA. She asked who I was.
SAL. What did you say?
JOSHUA. I said I'm his brother.
SAL. He's black!
JOSHUA. Don't be so close-minded!
SAL. Then who am I? His white, Irish sister?
JOSHUA. *(The answer.)* You're you.
SAL. *Oh, Okay.* So how much longer?
JOSHUA. Soon. *(Pause.)* They don't *want* to keep him here.
SAL. What do you know?
JOSHUA. I'm affiliated with a medical resident here in New York.
SAL. Who?
JOSHUA. My half-stepbrother.
SAL. *Half*-step?
JOSHUA. He and my stepfather do not qualify as *whole* people. There are too many basic human qualities that they're lacking.
SAL. Like?
JOSHUA. Besides humor and charisma? Loyalty and respect. Anyway, he's told me a little bit about working in the ER, the most common types of admissions, procedures, etc., as long as I could bear the conversation. In fact, if you ever meet him, just remember that we're not related.
SAL. Why?
JOSHUA. Because he's incredibly dry, technical, and completely socially inept.
SAL. What do you mean?
JOSHUA. His bedside manner could kill the patient!
SAL. Oh. I get it.
JOSHUA. *(To further prove his point.)* The only placement he could get was in the South Bronx! And they wouldn't even put him in the main hospital. They stuck him in this tiny pediatric emer-

gency room across the Grand Concourse from the main entrance! *(Sal is quiet. There is silence for a few beats.)* Anyway, I'm on a tangent. But this *is* pretty different from *ER.* No one's hooking up and getting busy with each other.

SAL. This isn't television.

JOSHUA. Lightfield auditioned for *Law and Order.*

SAL. Oh yeah?

JOSHUA. Yeah. The part was to play this kid who had just gotten shot. So he went in holding his chest with one of those fake blood pellets.

SAL. Did he get the part?

JOSHUA. No. Actually, they said he stained their carpet. *(Sal laughs a little bit. Trying to entertain her.)* Look I can act. *(He performs a dramatic mock death where he clutches at his throat and then ends up sprawled out on the floor. Sal laughs.)* I should be on that show.

SAL. You wouldn't be allowed. Your GPA's too low.

JOSHUA. So's yours.

SAL. I had substitute teachers.

JOSHUA. I skipped class.

SAL. I was put on the honors track.

JOSHUA. I was put in a peer-counseling consortium.

SAL. *(Casually.)* I have family problems.

JOSHUA. I have attention deficit disorder.

SAL. That's an understatement! *(Josh gets up from the floor. He sits one seat closer to Sal than he was before. There is a pause. A page for a doctor is heard.)*

JOSHUA. We're not going to tell anyone about this.

SAL. Fine.

JOSHUA. Keep it double-down. Lightfield did very well on his PSATs. He'll go to Yale if they give him financial aid.

SAL. I want to go there.

JOSHUA. You have to be more than just smart. You need a *hook.*

SAL. A hook?

JOSHUA. Yeah, a hook. Don't you know what a hook is?

SAL. Not really.

JOSHUA. Like fishing. The hook is like the thing that clinches the deal. You know? Like Lightfield's an actor. And he's black. He's a *black actor.* That's his hook. Like for instance, your hook could be that your mother carpools you to school in Manhattan! *(Sal punches him.)*

SAL. What's your hook? A dime bag?

JOSHUA. *(Proudly.)* I'm an expert chess player.
SAL. Were.
JOSHUA. I won my division. They flew me to Saratoga!
SAL. That was three years ago.
JOSHUA. I'm just waiting to get into the over-eighteens. I got sick of these eleven-year-old freaks in Harlem. I could barely see their heads over the table.
SAL. Sure.
JOSHUA. Do you know who Maurice Ashley is?
SAL. No.
JOSHUA. He's the highest-ranked black player in history. He does Tai Chi before a match. He says chess is intellectual karate. Don't fuck with me. *(Josh starts doing exaggerated, aggressive karate moves, but then slows down into more like Tai Chi.)*
SAL. Yeah right. You quit. Just say it.
JOSHUA. And what sets you apart? *(Sal hesitates.)*
SAL. I won the science fair?
JOSHUA. Oh right. You know, making a DNA model with ping-pong balls and pipe cleaners has been done before!
SAL. Shut up! Mr. Gardino says DNA is the future. He says one day people are going to be able to sell it … *(Josh looks at her quizzically for a moment.)*
JOSHUA. Well, if people can sell their DNA, then yours is lying on a blanket on Avenue A next to a rusty clock and some Parliament records.
SAL. I also do volunteering!
JOSHUA. Where?
SAL. At an AIDS clinic.
JOSHUA. What exactly do you do there?
SAL. Office work. I lick envelopes.
JOSHUA. Don't lick the wrong envelope!
SAL. I like it there.
JOSHUA. *(An announcement.)* I'm straight, you know.
SAL. Yes, you like to demonstrate that as much as you can …
JOSHUA. … none of this bisexual crap like everyone else in school.
SAL. … trying to meet that girl tonight …
JOSHUA. She was *fine*, that's why.
SAL. She wanted to meet *Lightfield! (Sal pauses. There is silence.)*
JOSHUA. I should call Farland.
SAL. *(Pointed.)* He's a lunatic. *(More silence. Sal looks at Josh.*

Defensively.) What?
JOSHUA. Nothing. *(He looks down at the seat next to him.)* Why would Lightfield pass on a girl like that?
SAL. Lightfield's gay.
JOSHUA. You're tripping!
SAL. He doesn't tell you because you're homophobic.
JOSHUA. He's not *gay.* Lightfield isn't a *gay name.*
SAL. *(Incredulously.) It's not?! (Josh doesn't answer. He dips his finger in the peanut butter again.)*
JOSHUA. Do you have any supersize Wonder Bread to go with the peanut butter?
SAL. *(Sarcastically.)* I don't know. Why don't you go look? *(They do more of nothing.)*
JOSHUA. I took Tai Chi once. But of all the martial arts, Maurice excluded, Tai Chi is definitely the one for the gay community.
SAL. What? Why do you say that?
JOSHUA. Maybe because the moves have names like "Grasp the Sparrow's Tail," "Part the Wild Horse's Mane," and "Play the Lute!" And the most questionable one is certainly "Repulse the Monkey." *(Sal doesn't respond.)* I get the point of it though, you know, the purpose. It's a practice of attaining peace through balance and continuous motion. It feels like you're moving through water. Like a baby in the womb. *(Sal still doesn't respond. They sit in silence for a few beats.)* I'm going to the bathroom. *(He takes off down the hall. Sal sits there for a moment, unsure of what to do. She takes the jar of peanut butter and dips her finger in right where Josh was eating from. She halfheartedly eats a little, then gives up and puts it away. Josh reenters and sits down.)*
SAL. How much longer? I really don't want to have to call my mom.
JOSHUA. The doctor's coming. Chill out.
SAL. I really don't want to have to call her.
JOSHUA. I wouldn't either. She's probably organized a neighborhood search party. With Tupperware. A Tupperware search party. Bring a casserole. And I'm not going to mention the *other* thing.
SAL. Shut up!
JOSHUA. I wouldn't do that to you.
SAL. I appreciate that.
JOSHUA. We have to think about Lightfield right now.
SAL. I agree.
JOSHUA. I don't want to get you upset.
SAL. Thank you.

JOSHUA. So is she still writing letters to the guy from "All My Children"?
SAL. You just said you weren't going to bring that up!
JOSHUA. C'mon.
SAL. When you were expounding upon your theory that my mother appropriates a middle-class suburban lifestyle right in the middle of Manhattan.
JOSHUA. Well, I would say watching a soap opera regularly supports that theory, wouldn't you?! Besides, I wouldn't call Yorkville the middle of Manhattan. It's tangential. It doesn't belong.
SAL. Speak for yourself!
JOSHUA. So is she still writing letters?
SAL. *(Does not want to talk about it.)* She did that once, okay? And it's not like it was fan mail. They met at a bookstore.
JOSHUA. Oh.
SAL. And besides, that was a good thing. At least she was out. She bought a photo album that day, and a cookbook. She was happy.
JOSHUA. I was just kidding.
SAL. Just lay off already. I don't want to think about her.
JOSHUA. I'm just teasing!
SAL. I go out at night so I can forget about her. I don't want to think about her face, and her television. I want to enjoy myself. It's bad enough when I get home at night and as soon as I put the key in the door I feel this complete sense of dread in the pit of my stomach. Like the air in my apartment is contaminated and I'm about to breathe it in again. *(There is a silence. A page for a doctor is heard. Josh starts to laugh.)* What's so funny?
JOSHUA. Spray some Glade.
SAL. You're such a jerk.
JOSHUA. I'm just kidding.
SAL. *(Not angry at him, but sad, confiding her frustration to him.)* What do you know? Your mom's with someone. She's happy. My mom barely goes out. She says she'd rather stay home and clean the apartment. I'm not even allowed to have friends over because they'll interfere with her depression. And she doesn't want to wash her hair. Sometimes she goes a whole week. I tell her that if maybe we had people around she would start to feel better. But she doesn't listen. She'll sit there watching "Jeopardy" and bad-mouth my dad. The same speech I've been hearing since he left. On and on and on and on. And then when he comes over to pick me up, she puts on lipstick! She doesn't wash her hair, and she has on the same outfit she's worn

for three days, but she puts on lipstick! I swear one night I'm going to go out, and I'm just not going to come home. *(They sit in silence for a few beats. Sal becomes embarrassed.)* I just don't want to have to call her. *(Pause.)* You don't realize how lucky you are. You do whatever you want. You could come home tomorrow and it's fine. I come home tomorrow and I'm on the back of a milk carton.
JOSHUA. Have you been on the back of one yet?
SAL. No.
JOSHUA. So calm down. *(Pause. Josh stands for a second, looks down the hallway, and then sits back down.)* Remember Eben Macauley? He disappeared. Or was kidnapped. One or the other. No one ever saw him again. One day in the summer between fourth and fifth grade I was riding around. I saw him standing outside 158 on York Avenue. He was doing the summer program and he was waiting for his mom to come get him. He had just gotten a haircut and I remember his scalp was really pink. And he was squinting his eyes, cause people with blond hair and blue eyes can't see in bright sunlight. I waved at him from my bike, and I said, "Yo Eben, what's up?" But he didn't hear me. So I kept going and looped around the block and when I passed the corner again he was gone. That was the last time I saw him. And a week later he disappeared. His parents mobilized the entire city. I think the mayor started a task force. There were posters on every bus. His father quit his job. Their lives completely stopped. The only thing they lived for was to find their son. They lived in the Pavillion. That building on 77th with the pool on the roof? I'd hung out with him a little bit in the summers, when we were younger. I would have dinner at his house. It was weird, the way the whole family sat down together, every night, at the table … They had this room, it had white linoleum floors, and toys in there and books. It faced the East River and at night the moon reflected off the water and the whole family would go in there after dinner. They called it the moonlight room.
SAL. I remember him. I remember seeing the signs on the buses.
JOSHUA. *(Pause.)* You can't help but wonder. Wonder what it is to wonder. Not knowing where he is or if he'll ever come home. What that must be like to live with every day. *(Josh looks away, thoughtfully. They are silent.)*
SAL. Is that where you went before Humanities? 158?
JOSHUA. Yeah, when we still lived on the East Side. Where did you go?
SAL. Ethical Culture.

JOSHUA. You went to *Ethical Culture* before *Humanities,* and you're this fucked up?
SAL. I'm not fucked up!
JOSHUA. You're morally bankrupt.
SAL. No I'm not. That implies someone with no values at all.
JOSHUA. No! It implies someone who used to have values and lost them.
SAL. I have values.
JOSHUA. You saw your own mother on the subway once and didn't say hello.
SAL. That's because she was still teaching then and she was with her class.
JOSHUA. Why were they on the subway anyway?
SAL. Because they were on a class trip. They were going to the Botanical Gardens.
JOSHUA. So you booked into another car?
SAL. She was with a class full of third graders. It would have set them off!
JOSHUA. Nice. Your own mother. Running away from her.
SAL. Leave me alone. I do my best.
JOSHUA. So name one thing you value.
SAL. *(Glaring at him.)* Friendship!
JOSHUA. *Friendship?*
SAL. *I* value our friendship.
JOSHUA. Would you give your life to save mine?
SAL. I don't know.
JOSHUA. Then you don't value our friendship.
SAL. Would you do it for Lightfield?
JOSHUA. He's my best friend.
SAL. Answer the question.
JOSHUA. I did. *(Sal is about to respond but then stops herself. An abrupt shift.)* I'm calling Farland.
SAL. What did he do tonight?
JOSHUA. They went to a show at Irving Plaza.
SAL. *(Sarcastically.)* They didn't want to drive out to Hoboken? *(Josh gets up and goes to the pay phone. He puts in a quarter and then dials Farland's cell phone number. He gets a voicemail, so he punches in the pay phone's number, and then hangs up. He returns to his seat.)*
JOSHUA. We have to be there for Lightfield, you know? When they're done. He's going to be upset. *(With the sound of footsteps approaching, Josh and Sal look down the hallway. Then the footsteps stop.)*

SAL. *Damn!*

JOSHUA. I know, we didn't get to hear the second set.

SAL. No, I mean, I thought that was the doctor!

JOSHUA. Oh. *(The phone rings. Josh jumps up to answer it.)* Farland! … Yeah … I'm with Sal … Yeah … It's not a good scene actually. We're at New York Hospital, at the emergency room. With Lightfield … Yep … Un-huh … No he was fine at first and then he went backstage right before they went on … Some band he knows through his movie friends … 'Cause they were *playing* in Hoboken! … And then when he came out he was with us. And then all of a sudden a half hour later he said that we should stay but he wanted to leave. He was in a hole. He was going to take the PATH train but we said no … Because you don't take the *PATH train* in a *hole!* So we put him in Sal's car and … yeah her mom has a car … yeah in *New York!* … I know I think it's weird too … and then he just passed out. And we could barely wake him … No not too long, about an hour. Yeah I'm sure it will … Yeah I know I heard that one too … Where will you be later? … Do you know where you'll be? If I need to make a move … Really? She's fine! I hope it goes well … Cool, I'll hit you in an hour … Or call me at this number! Yeah it's a pay phone. Yeah I will … Later … *(He is about to hang up but then he remembers something.)* Oh wait! How was the show? *(But Farland has hung up. Joshua hangs up the phone.)* He says we did the right thing. And just to call him later and let him know how he's doing. He doesn't think it should take too long. He says it will be fine.

SAL. He's not coming?

JOSHUA. There's no need. It's under control. He knows that kid too.

SAL. Who?

JOSHUA. Sajit. *(Blackout.)*

Scene 2

Lights up. The waiting room. In between Sal and Josh sits a middle-aged woman in her early forties (Mrs. Kelly). She is as Sal described her: unwashed hair, messy clothes. She looks homeless. She was clearly once very beautiful. Josh and Mrs. Kelly are in mid-conversation. They seem to be getting along very well, as if they're old friends. Sal listens miserably.

JOSHUA. He's the youngest player ever to compete in the majors.
MRS. KELLY. Tiger Woods is.
JOSHUA. No. The other kid.
MRS. KELLY. Sergio Garcia.
JOSHUA. *(Excited.)* Yes! He's incredible. He swings with his eyes closed. He doesn't need to look at the hole. He just senses where to aim. He's a genius.
SAL. You mean a prodigy.
MRS. KELLY. And he's only nineteen?
JOSHUA. That's all. But Tiger still won the tournament.
MRS. KELLY. Which one?
JOSHUA. The PGA.
MRS. KELLY. What does that stand for?
JOSHUA. Parental Guidance Assassinated.
MRS. KELLY. What!?
JOSHUA. *(All charm.)* Just kidding. Pro Golf Association.
SAL. *(Pointedly.)* Why are we discussing *golf* right now?
JOSHUA. *(Pointedly.)* It's a pastime.
SAL. *(Snapping.)* Maybe we should all just be quiet.
MRS. KELLY. Lose your attitude, miss. *(Josh laughs out loud. Sal sits back in her chair, horrified.)*
JOSHUA. Do you have any magazines?
MRS. KELLY. I have the *Enquirer* and the *Star*.
JOSHUA. Is there a difference?
MRS. KELLY. They cover different events.
JOSHUA. Like …
SAL. Josh!
MRS. KELLY. I don't mind. *(Simply.)* The *Enquirer* focuses on

world events, alien contact, natural disasters, and the *Star* is more celebrity-focused.

JOSHUA. Oh.

SAL. Reading a magazine right now doesn't seem appropriate to me.

JOSHUA. Really? What else are we going to do?

MRS. KELLY. Well, I think we all need to sit here and wait in a considerate manner.

JOSHUA. I agree.

SAL. He's not very good at that. *(They are all silent for a few beats.)*

JOSHUA. Is anyone hungry? *(No one answers. Sal glares at him.)* I mean I could really use something. Like a sandwich? Some peanut butter …

MRS. KELLY. I'm sure there's a snack bar.

SAL. You mean a cafeteria? This isn't a theme park.

JOSHUA. There must be, right?

MRS. KELLY. I would think so.

JOSHUA. 'Cause I have an appetite for chronic.

MRS. KELLY. Excuse me? *(Sal shoots Josh a look.)*

JOSHUA. I have a chronic appetite.

MRS. KELLY. *(Perplexed.)* Oh.

SAL. *(Through gritted teeth.)* If you're going to go just go! *(Josh gets up.)*

JOSHUA. Okay, I'm going.

SAL. *Okay! (Josh exits.)* Mom. Don't do this to me.

MRS. KELLY. What did I do?

SAL. "Lose your attitude, miss."

MRS. KELLY. I'm sorry.

SAL. Please don't humiliate me.

MRS. KELLY. I'm your mother. It's part of the job description.

SAL. What do you need to bring your magazines for?

MRS. KELLY. I had them in my purse.

SAL. That's tacky.

MRS. KELLY. Don't criticize.

SAL. It's embarrassing.

MRS. KELLY. You have more to worry about than that right now. Watch yourself. I'll be the only friend you've got.

SAL. *(Sarcastic.)* That's not saying much. *(Josh reenters.)*

JOSHUA. It's not open at night.

MRS. KELLY. It's after three. Does your mother know where you are?

JOSHUA. She's fine.

SAL. Josh can do what he wants. *They* have a very good relationship.

MRS. KELLY. Then why isn't she sitting here with you?
SAL. What is this, Parents' Day?
MRS. KELLY. Well it sounds like your friend is in a lot of pain.
JOSHUA. *(Confused.)* He can't feel it.
MRS. KELLY. Appendicitis is very painful.
JOSHUA. *(Looks at Sal amused.)* Interesting! … That's true, actually. Appendicitis is very painful. But, he's going to be fine. And hopefully soon, we'll all be able to go home. It's too bad Sal had to wake you.
MRS. KELLY. I was up.
JOSHUA. At three in the morning?
MRS. KELLY. We have an agreement. She has to be home by three. If I wake up at three and she's not home, I panic.
SAL. *(Pleading.)* Mom, maybe you should just go home.
MRS. KELLY. Not as long as you're still here, miss.
SAL. *(Horrified.)* Oh God.
JOSHUA. Do you have, like, an alarm set? I mean how do you wake up?
MRS. KELLY. What parent do you know that is able to sleep while their child is out in this city?
JOSHUA. *(Cheerfully.)* Mine!
SAL. Don't refer to me as a child!
MRS. KELLY. You really should call your mom.
JOSHUA. It's fine.
SAL. Mom, just drive the car home. I'll be home in twenty minutes. I'll take a cab.
MRS. KELLY. Not on your life.
SAL. You're so overprotective!
MRS. KELLY. *Overprotective?!* That's easy for you to say, from where you're sitting. Do you have any idea what parents go through? *(Not making fun of her daughter or condemning her. Simply describing a routine that's ultimately a lonely one.)* First it's the telephone marathon. Every Friday and Saturday night she camps out on the floor of the kitchen and talks on the phone for two hours. Whose house is having the party tonight? What doorman is working what club? Who is going out with who? Who's wearing what? And she makes her plans. And then she spends hours getting ready. She dries her hair so much the fuse in the apartment blows. She puts on makeup, takes it off, puts it on again. She puts clothes on, takes them off, puts them on again. She yells at me when she can't find something. She apologizes when she finds it. But I don't mind,

I want her to enjoy herself. To be happy—

SAL. *(Pleading, in absolute agony.)* Mom!

MRS. KELLY. — and then she walks out the door and I can hear her waiting for the elevator in the hallway. And I can hear the elevator doors open and close behind her … And then there's this silence. You can hear the hum of every electric appliance in the building. Refrigerators, track lighting, television sets. You can hear cars pulling up fifteen stories below … *(There is an awkward pause. Sal is about to die of embarrassment.)*

SAL. MOM, CUT IT OUT! *(Mrs. Kelly sadly looks at Sal. She wants to respond but can't. She's embarrassed. She gets up. Mrs. Kelly exits. There is an awkward moment.)*

JOSHUA. You told your mother he has appendicitis!

SAL. What was I supposed to say?

JOSHUA. You shouldn't have let her come here in the first place. You should have just gone home.

SAL. I wasn't going to leave you here! And you won't call his dad.

JOSHUA. I didn't think we needed parental involvement.

SAL. Then tell me what's happening!

JOSHUA. I *told* you. They're pumping his stomach.

SAL. That's *all* the doctor said?

JOSHUA. No. He said they're giving him a "gastric lavage." I didn't know you spoke French. *(Sal looks at him like he's hopeless.)* They put a plastic tube down his GI track and try to flush out pill fragments, even though I tried to tell them he didn't take pills, he took it in a powder. But as the doctor condescendingly explained to me, there isn't an existing toxic screen for Ketamine, so therefore they can't rule out anything, they can only "suspect" Ketamine, so what I tell them is practically worthless. So in the same tube they "lavaged" him with, they give him something called "activated charcoal" to bind to the remaining substances in question. They're also giving him something called Narcan which is meant to counteract the effects of opiodes. Okay? That's what they told me. You shouldn't have belittled the situation by telling your mom it was his appendix.

SAL. I didn't "belittle" the situation. I legalized it. There's a difference.

JOSHUA. Are you comparing a drug overdose to appendicitis?

SAL. *(Pointedly.)* No. Friends don't help friends get appendicitis.

JOSHUA. *(Earnest for the first time.)* I had nothing to do with it! *(The pay phone begins to ring. Josh dashes for the phone and picks it up.)* Farland?! … Farland? *(But there is nobody there. Dejectedly,*

Joshua hangs up the phone.) Jesus. Who would of thought we'd end up here tonight.
SAL. I know.
JOSHUA. I was born in this hospital.
SAL. Me too. *(There is a pause. Josh gently puts his arm around Sal. At the same time both proud and surprised that it's there. They sit like that for a few moments.)*
JOSHUA. *(Trying to be helpful.)* I see what you mean about your mom. She clearly hasn't joined the psychopharmacological revolution. So you know what? Tomorrow I'm just going to come over and she will have to deal with it. She's just going to have to get used to having people around. She needs to get broken in. She's like a dog that needs training.
SAL. *(Skeptical.)* Thanks. Anyway, I don't know.
JOSHUA. You'll see. It will be fine. *(Sal doesn't respond, but considers the idea. They wait in silence for a while. Finally Josh stands restlessly.)* They never found him.
SAL. Who?
JOSHUA. Eben Macauley. *(He pauses.)* Did you know that there are almost three-quarters of a million cases of missing children each year? They get divided into two categories: "Involuntary" and "Endangered." "Involuntary" means missing under circumstances indicating that the disappearance was not voluntary, like an abduction or a kidnapping. "Endangered" refers to a missing child in the company of another person under circumstances indicating that his or her physical or emotional well-being is in danger.
SAL. I didn't know that. *(Josh pauses, his mind elsewhere.)*
JOSHUA. *(Darkly.)* Now here's the real crazy thing. Did you know that there's a connection between missing children and tap dancing? May twenty-fifth is National Missing Children's Day *and* National Tap Dance Day! Can you believe that? And that the National Center for Missing Kids and The National Tap Dance Association actually teamed up last year for a *Tap Dance Festival?* They called it "Tap 2002," to *educate* and *entertain* people on the subject of missing children. Can you believe that … *(He starts to shuffle, and then goes into a times step.)*
SAL. Josh …
JOSHUA. Can you believe that?!
SAL. *(Wanting him to stop before her mother gets back.)* Josh! *(Josh's tap dancing has become Motown–style slides and turns.)*
JOSHUA. *(Singing.)* "You make me feel like dancing … gonna

dance the night away … " *(He tries to pull her up out of her seat as he continues to dance. Suddenly, Mrs. Kelly enters from the direction of the nurses station. Josh stops dancing immediately. Mrs. Kelly looks at him like he is from another planet and then glares at Sal. She has been clued in on the situation.)*
MRS. KELLY. Can you step outside? I'd like to have a word with you. *(Sal and her mom exit. Josh sits down nervously for a few beats. He then gets up and puts a quarter in the pay phone and pages Farland. He sits down and waits. A page for a doctor is called. The sounds of ambulances outside. Finally the phone rings. Josh runs and picks it up.)*
JOSHUA. *(Panicked.)* Hi … Yeah, I am … No, actually it's taken a turn for the worse … *worse!* … I'm sorry I didn't know you heard me … I don't know what to do … They've probably called his dad by now … I told the doctor everything I know … No, I didn't do that! … I don't know what else … I don't know, he was backstage … I didn't … *I didn't.* So what's your plan? … Really? So maybe I could come meet up? … *That well, huh?!* … I won't bust in the way … It's just I *gotta* make a move … okay … okay … it's fine. Later. *(He hangs up the phone and sits down. He puts his head in his hands. Suddenly, the sound of footsteps approaching from stage right. Josh shifts in his seat uncomfortably. He quickly glances at the approaching figure, and then looks away. A black man in his late forties walks onto the stage. He is dressed in a sweater and a pair of slacks. He looks at Josh for a long and uncomfortable moment. And then he sits down. Blackout.)*

Scene 3

Lights up on the waiting area. It is now almost daylight outside. Sal is curled up across two seats, trying to sleep. Josh is sitting in the last seat of the row, trying to keep to himself. Mrs. Kelly and Mr. Wells are in the middle of a conversation. Mr. Wells is clearly distraught. Mrs. Kelly tries to console him.

MRS. KELLY. She wanted to do everything with me. If I needed to run down to the store for cigarettes, she wanted to come. If I was going downstairs to put more quarters in the machine, she would fol-

low me. We tried to put her in nursery school, she wouldn't hear of it. One summer we tried day camp but she wouldn't get on the bus.
MR. WELLS. *(Slowly, soulfully.)* She wouldn't get on the bus.
MRS. KELLY. Separation anxiety, they said. Some children have it acutely. She doesn't have it anymore.
MR. WELLS. That's right. Doing their own thing.
MRS. KELLY. Well, Lightfield's very independent.
MR. WELLS. *(Takes a long, deep sigh.)* Well, he has his career. He's very dedicated to the acting. And they seem to want him for a lot of things. His mother used to take him on his appointments. But now he wants to go on his own. Legally he's allowed to be at work without a guardian but my sister goes from time to time. I don't go very often.
JOSHUA. *(Piping in.)* I went with you once. *(Suddenly, Mr. Wells' quiet demeanor turns to pure hatred. He glares over at Josh.)*
MR. WELLS. Did somebody speak?! *(Josh shuts up.)* I didn't think so.
MRS. KELLY. When do you think your sister will get here?
MR. WELLS. Well, she's coming in from Edison. She's driving. I spoke to her about thirty-five minutes ago, so I'm assuming it won't take her much longer.
MRS. KELLY. No, it shouldn't.
MR. WELLS. Not too long. *(He puts his face in his hands for a moment. Then he stands up. There is an awkward pause. Trying to contain his frustration.)* They're bringing in another doctor. He's not reacting yet to anything. They don't know the whole story …
JOSHUA. I told the doctor everything. *(Again, Mr. Wells glares at Josh like he could kill him without getting out of his seat.)*
MR. WELLS. Thank you for that information that we've heard from you fifty times already! If you don't mind your presence is offensive to me enough. *(Again, Josh shuts up. Sal sleepily lifts her head. She looks around disoriented. She gets up and starts to head to the vending machine. She looks at Josh.)*
SAL. Do you want anything? *(Josh is about to answer but then he thinks better of it. He shakes his head meekly, not wanting any attention called to him.)*
MR. WELLS. There's just no excuse for this. There was an incident at his party this year, involving substances brought along by a certain guest *(He pauses to glare at Josh.)* and two things were made clear. Number one, that a habit of any kind would not be tolerated. And number two, that a certain individual *(He pauses again to glare at Josh.)* was not supposed to be anywhere in the vicinity of my son.

And somehow, here we are … *(At that moment, a nurse motions to Mr. Wells from offstage.)* Excuse me. *(He gets up and follows the nurse out hurriedly stage right. Sal returns to her seat with her soda.)*
JOSHUA. Mrs. Kelly?
MRS. KELLY. What?
JOSHUA. When are we going to know something?
MRS. KELLY. *(Rudely, her whole attitude towards Josh has now changed.)* You heard him. They're bringing in another doctor.
SAL. I don't understand. It's all so sudden.
MRS. KELLY. Sudden? You've been here since one in the morning. I would say that there has been a slow and steady progression for the worse.
JOSHUA. *(Under his breath.)* It's certainly progressed from appendicitis.
MRS. KELLY. What did you say?
JOSHUA. Nothing. *(Suddenly the pay phone rings. Josh jumps out of his seat to grab it. Mrs. Kelly eyes him suspiciously. Josh picks up the phone.)* Farland! … What's going on …
MRS. KELLY. How does he know who it is?
SAL. He paged someone.
MRS. KELLY. What does that mean?
SAL. He called somebody's cell phone and they're calling him back.
MRS. KELLY. How?
SAL. *(Exasperated.)* Do I have to explain everything to you?
JOSHUA. *(On the phone.)* I thought it was going so well … man … you got blocked … YOU GOT BLOCKED … you know what it means … I can't say the full word right now … because I am in the presence of someone who isn't going to want to hear it … FINE … take the word blocked and put the word for a male chicken in front of it … Whoa … E.Z. brother … Yeah I know who he is … Who told you that? Really … Are you sure? … Yeah … I've been there, it's in the park, you take the 106th entrance … what time? … I really don't know … c'mon cuz, that's going a little far … *(Josh puts the phone down and looks at Sal and her mother. He notices for the first time that they are glaring at him.)* I got to go. I'll try. *(He hangs up the phone.)*
SAL. What is going on?
JOSHUA. *(Visibly nervous.)* He … um … well there was the girl he was with, but you know that kid Frank Sanchez? He moved in, completely, and now *(He tries to keep his voice down so Mrs. Kelly can't hear.)* he's going to meet this kid X-Ray so he can buy a —

MRS. KELLY. *(Loudly.)* Stop whispering.
JOSHUA. … piece.
SAL. Oh God.
MRS. KELLY. What?
JOSHUA. *(To Mrs. Kelly.)* Peace. *(He holds up two fingers for the peace sign in Mrs. Kelly's direction. She looks at him confused. To Sal.)* He's flipping out. I've never heard him this angry.
SAL. He's a lunatic. He was arrested three times last year. You shouldn't even hang out with him.
MRS. KELLY. *(Interrupting.)* Who are you talking about? *(To Josh.)* You know, you are clearly the type of person that attracts trouble. It's written all over your face.
JOSHUA. Have you met many of Sal's friends?
SAL. Josh!
MRS. KELLY. No, but …
JOSHUA. I didn't think so.
SAL. *(Uncomfortable.)* Josh!
MRS. KELLY. Are you judging me? Who do you think you are? To judge me. You're the whole reason this has happened. Your friend is in critical condition. *Critical!* And you're judging me? You have trouble all over your face.
JOSHUA. *(Really getting into the argument.)* I've heard that one before. Try to come up with something original!
SAL. *(Getting very upset.)* Josh you're fighting with my mom! Fighting. Stop it!
MRS. KELLY. You've heard it before because it's true. You're the whole reason for this mess. And if you think you're going to ever see my daughter again you are duly mistaken. *(Suddenly another page for a doctor is heard, and there is a commotion from offstage. Josh stands up terrified, as if anticipating what's to come.)*
JOSHUA. I'm going to go outside and get some air. *(He exits. Sal looks at her mother, distraught.)*
MRS. KELLY. You better cut it out right now. This is some mess you're in and you better hold it together. I am running out of patience with you and this whole situation. When Mr. Wells comes back I'm going to tell him we're leaving. We shouldn't even be here. This is a family situation now. This is a family situation. *(Mrs. Kelly stands up and begins to collect her things. Sal reaches to touch her mom's arm, to try to reason with her. But Mrs. Kelly abruptly yanks her arm away.)*
SAL. Mom, please. It's not my fault.
MRS. KELLY. What are you talking about? You're in a hospital

right now! Look at the situation you're in … On your birthday, no less. *(Sal doesn't say anything. Suddenly the sound of footsteps approaching from offstage. Sal stands, increasingly nervous.)*

SAL. *(Pleading.)* Mom, c'mon. We have to stay a little longer. I can't just leave, okay? It's not right. And then I'll just go home and worry!

MRS. KELLY. Don't be ridiculous! Let me give you a piece of advice. You better go find this person and tell him that if he knows what's good for him he'll get out of here.

SAL. Please don't make me! I don't want to go! I love him.

MRS. KELLY. What are you talking about?!

SAL. I'm not going!

MRS. KELLY. What?!

SAL. *You don't understand!*

MRS. KELLY. I am running out of patience! You're not being reasonable. It's time for us to leave!

SAL. *(Blurts out.)* I don't want to go *with you! (Mrs. Kelly stares at Sal, silenced, for a few beats. She looks broken. Sal gets up and runs out of the waiting room. Mr. Wells enters the waiting area.)*

MRS. KELLY. Mr. Wells? *(Mr. Wells is silent. He sits and puts his head in his hands for a long, uncomfortable moment. Mrs. Kelly sits quietly next to him. Weakly.)* Mr. Wells? Any news?

MR. WELLS. *(Stoic, resigned.)* I worked with this man on a job, and his son also worked construction. They usually worked together but one time they were at different sites. And his son was erecting this scaffolding and the structure collapsed, and it killed him. And I was with his father when he found out. We had just gotten our lunch and he had just unwrapped his sandwich and then suddenly the foreman came running up and told him about the accident, and there was this whole commotion. And he started screaming and someone drove up in a car and took him away. And the whole afternoon I just kept staring at the unwrapped white paper of his sandwich, uneaten. And I just kept thinking that that sandwich was the last thing he had looked at before his whole life fell apart. The last innocent thing. I couldn't bring myself to pick it up and throw it away. I left it there the whole afternoon. But now here I am, see? My son is fighting for his life. *(Mrs. Kelly nods sadly. Mr. Wells exits the waiting area. Mrs. Kelly stands and closes her coat. Sal enters, shivering. All the color has left her face.)*

SAL. *(Quietly.)* I can't find him.

MRS. KELLY. We're leaving. *(From the tone of her voice, Sal does not have any options. She collects her jacket slowly, and puts it on, as if in a daze. They exit. The stage is empty. The pay phone rings but no one is there to answer it. A few more moments pass. Josh enters. He paces nervously, and then goes to the phone. He puts in a quarter and dials.)*

JOSHUA. It's me … I'm fine. I'm just wondering if you've changed your mind … *I'm just wondering* … Because I thought you might … I've stopped all that … Well how are you supposed to know if I'm not allowed in the house? … You don't know that I've changed because you haven't seen me … You haven't seen me because I'm not allowed in the house … It's not reverse psychology, it's deductive logic … No, I'm just trying to reason with you. There is a difference between living at home and disappearing for days and not living at home at all … Because those things are exactly what I don't do anymore … Obviously we don't agree … Well I thought maybe you'd changed your mind … No, *Mom,* you've made it abundantly clear … Fine! *(Josh hangs up the phone. He sits down in a panic and then stands again. Mr. Wells enters the waiting area. He sees Josh and approaches him and looks at him as if he wants to kill him. He's almost in a trance. Josh is terrified.)* I'm leaving … I'm leaving … Okay? I know you don't want to see my face. *(Mr. Wells' body relaxes, just slightly.)* Do you know what time it is? Is it close to seven? *(Suddenly, Mr. Wells grabs Josh by each shoulder, sharply, and looks at him intently, as if he can't even find the words.)*

MR. WELLS. What have you done? What have you done?! *(Mr. Wells starts to shake him. This is not a violent act, but a man who is losing the ability to contain his anguish. He does not mean to hurt him. Josh tries to fight it at first but then his body goes limp. Josh's small frame looks as if it might snap in two. Suddenly, Mr. Wells stops and lets go of Josh. He comes to his senses. He stares at Josh as if he's seeing him for the first time. As if he is his own son. Josh moves away and struggles for something to say.)*

JOSHUA. *(Nervously.)* The last tournament I played … I was really stuck. I had lost my queen too early and my opponent knew it and he was going to win. He had his king on the F file and his queen at the bottom of the G. And I kept telling myself don't move until you feel it, don't move until you feel it. Because chess is not a game and it's not a science, it's instinct. Right? It's nature. So I pushed my pawn forward on the file and got another queen. I come in on the E and I get to give the first check, right? So I move to the F file and he moves his king out of check to G6. But if I follow him there, he'll have to move back and his queen will be exposed. So I slide to G8, he moves back to the F, and I skewer him into a setup check and capture his queen. And I hit my clock and I knew I pushed through, right? I pushed through. *(Brief pause.)* He'll push through, I promise. *(Mr. Wells just stares at him. After a beat, Josh grabs his backpack and runs out of the waiting area and exits. Mr. Wells stands on the stage alone, almost unable to move. The lights go dim. Blackout.)*

End of Act One

ACT TWO

Scene 1

Lights up on the waiting room. It is early afternoon. Sal sits on one of the orange chairs by herself. She does not look like she has slept at all, and she is agitated, restless. She wears the same clothes as the day before. She gets up, goes to the pay phone, puts in a quarter and punches in a number. She sits down, hopeless.

SAL. *(To herself.)* This isn't happening. *(She waits. A young man enters the waiting area. He is in his late twenties, medium build, and kind of nondescript looking, except for an overwhelming and definitely off-putting dorky quality. He speaks technically, factually. Devoid of emotion. He sits down next to Sal.)* Did you look upstairs?
ADAM. Yeah.
SAL. Did you look outside?
ADAM. Yeah.
SAL. But he told you to meet him here?
ADAM. When I got done with my shift. Yeah.
SAL. *(Sighing.)* Okay. *(There is a long silence. A page for a doctor is heard.)*
ADAM. *(Eagerly.)* So we were talking about?
SAL. *(Thinly disguised dread.)* Um … Brain herniation?
ADAM. Brain herniation. Right. *(Adam takes a dramatic pause for effect. He clears his throat, and then picks up where they left off.)* So the nervous system controls your airway tone and your ability to protect your airway …
SAL. From?
ADAM. From saliva or vomit getting into your trachea and choking you, or into your lungs in which case you can get aspiration pneumonia.
SAL. Okay.
ADAM. And your breathing is mediated by your brain stem, so

therefore it is possible to lose consciousness and respiratory drive ...
SAL. Respiratory drive?
ADAM. Breathing. *(Adam pauses. Sal stares at him blankly.)*
SAL. Oh right.
ADAM. So along with the cardiovascular effects, there is also the possibility of toniclonic seizure, which is an uncontrolled series of electrical responses; intermittent hypertension, i.e., high blood pressure; a dystonic reaction — I'm not going to go into that — that's a problem with your muscles; and the polyneuropathic aspects.
SAL. Polyneuropathic?
ADAM. That involves the functioning of peripheral nerves not in your brain — you know when you feel weak or a strange sensation jetting down your legs or in your fingertips? *(Sal nods weakly.)* And the reason for all this, all these brain dysfunctions that disturb your central nervous system, is the increased intercranial pressure — that's pressure in your skull —
SAL. Okay.
ADAM. — which is due to the fact that Ketamine interferes with your brain's ability to reabsorb your cerebral spinal fluid. See, your brain is surrounded by fluid which is constantly reabsorbed by your brain. Does that make sense? *(Sal nods emphatically. In closing.)* So if your brain can't reabsorb your CSF quickly enough, due to the inhibiting effects of the drugs, the pressure will continue building in your skull, and therein lies the serious risk of brain herniation, which means basically that your brain is getting squeezed out of your skull and has begun to herniate. *(There is an awkward pause.)*
SAL. What does it mean?
ADAM. It means basically that your brain is getting squeezed out of your skull and has begun to herniate.
SAL. Oh!
ADAM. Do you have any questions?
SAL. Yes, I have a question. *(Sal clears her throat.)*
ADAM. What is it?
SAL. Um ... do you want something to drink? *(Pause.)* 'Cause I feel suddenly, I don't know, thirsty.
ADAM. No thanks. *(Sal stands up. Sal goes upstage to the vending machine.)* I'm just trying to explain the pathophysiology of the situation.
SAL. *(From upstage.)* I understand.
ADAM. In layman's terms. *(Sal returns to her seat with a soda. She*

looks at him dubiously.)

SAL. Those were layman's terms?

ADAM. *(Arrogantly.)* I left out stuff like parodoxical direct myocardial depression.

SAL. *(With a halfhearted laugh.)* Oh. Right. *(There is silence. Sal drinks her soda.)*

ADAM. So are you interested in medicine?

SAL. Not really.

ADAM. Have you taken any science?

SAL. *(Stating the obvious.)* I'm in high school!

ADAM. Have you responded to any of it? Physics … chemistry …

SAL. I kind of liked biology.

ADAM. What about exactly?

SAL. Um … DNA?

ADAM. Very glamorous. *(Sal looks at him likes he's crazy.)*

SAL. How so?

ADAM. Biotech. That's where we're at.

SAL. Do you know much about it?

ADAM. A lot.

SAL. I don't. I guess.

ADAM. DNA is deoxyribonucleic acid that contains the genetic information found in most organisms. It's made up of two polynucleotide chains that wind around each other to form a double helix structure, which are held together by hydrogen bonding …

SAL. *(Interrupting.)* You don't need to … um … explain the molecular structure to me! All I meant is that it's pretty amazing, when you think about it, the idea of your own *genetic code.*

ADAM. Genetic code refers to the formula by which the nucleotide sequence in DNA determines the amino acid sequence in proteins …

SAL. Oh … I kind of thought it meant that the secret of everything about you, who you are, is hidden in it. Your whole life, your whole future.

ADAM. That is not entirely *(Pause.)* correct.

SAL. Oh.

ADAM. On a basic level, a lot of factors play into who you are. Environment, conditioning … nature vs. — *(Suddenly Mrs. Kelly enters from stage right interrupting them. She is carrying a plastic container with a sandwich in it. She hands it to Sal and pays no attention to Adam as she assumes he is a total stranger.)*

MRS. KELLY. *(Very annoyed.)* Goddamnit! That cafeteria is a

crowded mess. I spent twenty minutes trying to get you a goddamn sandwich!
ADAM. *(To Sal, ironically.)* — nurture. *(There is an awkward pause. Mrs. Kelly sits down and settles into her seat on the other side of Sal. Sal looks at her sandwich with no intention of eating it.)* I didn't know your mother was here.
SAL. Yeah. Actually, she *is.* Mr. Wells called and asked us to come back.
ADAM. *(Standing up.)* Hello, Mrs. Kelly. I'm Dr. Adam Levy.
MRS. KELLY. Oh. Nice to meet you. I'm Sal's mother.
ADAM. I'm Josh's stepbrother.
MRS. KELLY. Oh. *(Pause.)* Hm.
ADAM. I'm just explaining to Sal the situation they were in last night so she can understand it better.
MRS. KELLY. Thank you.
ADAM. Luckily it sounds like things could turn around.
MRS. KELLY. Hopefully. Mr. Wells called and asked us to come back. He said there'd been some news.
ADAM. Thank God.
MRS. KELLY. You can only hope. It's a parent's worst nightmare …
ADAM. That it is.
MRS. KELLY. … the phone call in the middle of the night.
ADAM. *(Agreeing.)* Right. Well luckily it seems like things might turn around. These situations are highly unpredictable. I tried to explain that to Josh when he called last night that if the patient was non-responsive when he was admitted, there are certain procedures that they would do but —
SAL. What did you just say?
ADAM. That if the patient was nonresponsive when he was—
SAL. *(Interrupting.)* No, I mean, you said you spoke to Josh last night?
ADAM. He paged me to a pay phone.
SAL. What time?
ADAM. Around two or three in the morning.
SAL. *(Confused.)* But I was with him.
ADAM. He was out getting cigarettes. He said that they wouldn't tell him anything.
SAL. Was that last night or this morning?
ADAM. Last night. I didn't talk to him this morning.
SAL. I thought you said you told him you would come here when you got done with your shift?

ADAM. I did. My shift started yesterday.
SAL. *(Incredulous.)* It did?
ADAM. Yeah. *(He pauses.)* Do you know anything about being a medical resident?
SAL. Not really.
ADAM. Well your shifts go on for over twenty-four hours.
SAL. Oh. *(Really confused.)* So did you talk to him *last night* or *this morning?*
ADAM. Last night. I didn't talk to him this morning.
SAL. Oh. *(Concerned, this is bad news.)* So you haven't talked to him today at all?
ADAM. No. I spoke to him last night. I told him what the basic procedures for those kinds of admissions, you know your friend's situation: lavaging the patient, activated charcoal, etc.
SAL. *(Very preoccupied.)* Right.
ADAM. I wish there was more I could have done. I tried to call the hospital and speak to the on-call physician but I didn't have much luck.
SAL. They weren't very helpful.
ADAM. To be honest I am surprised that Josh called me.
SAL. *(Ironic.)* Me too.
ADAM. I don't get much opportunity to be a brother to him.
SAL. It's definitely clear that you both are not related.
ADAM. No, I mean, he hates me. My father too.
SAL. Oh, right.
ADAM. He said we don't even qualify as people.
SAL. *(Feigning surprise.)* He said that?
ADAM. He doesn't give us much of a chance, though. He's difficult to get a hold on, always coming and going as he pleases. They never know where he is or what he's doing. In terms of relationships in the family, it's difficult. I mean a family is a structure, everyone has to do their part. *(There is a pause.)*
MRS. KELLY. *(To Sal.)* Are you going to eat that?
SAL. Maybe later.
MRS. KELLY. Eat it now.
SAL. I don't have an appetite!
MRS. KELLY. Why not?
SAL. Considering the events of the last twenty-four hours?! *(To Adam.)* Adam, in your medical opinion, does it make sense that I don't have an appetite?
MRS. KELLY. Don't involve him. *(Adam's pager starts to vibrate in*

his pocket. He takes out a pager and a cell phone.)
ADAM. *(Distracted by his page.)* I … Uh, excuse me. *(Adam exits the waiting area. Sal is left alone with her mother.)*
MRS. KELLY. Where did he go?
SAL. He got a page.
MRS. KELLY. I didn't hear anything.
SAL. It's on vibrate!
MRS. KELLY. Huh?
SAL. *(Sick of having to explain this stuff to her.)* Oh Jesus!
MRS. KELLY. What is wrong with you?
SAL. What? Now what have I done?
MRS. KELLY. You've been acting especially strange all day.
SAL. No I haven't.
MRS. KELLY. Yes you have.
SAL. What's *especially* strange?
MRS. KELLY. You're restless.
SAL. So?
MRS. KELLY. You cleaned the apartment!
SAL. All I did was vacuum!
MRS. KELLY. Were you expecting somebody?
SAL. I just felt like vacuuming. That's all.
MRS. KELLY. Why?
SAL. I don't know. The carpet looked dirty?
MRS. KELLY. Define "dirty."
SAL. There are stains in it.
MRS. KELLY. Goddamnit!
SAL. What?!
MRS. KELLY. You don't get stains out by vacuuming. There isn't some magic detergent in it. You have to get it done professionally.
SAL. Well then maybe someone could come do it.
MRS. KELLY. Talk to your father about that? Okay? There's a whole list of things that need to get done. The apartment is falling apart.
SAL. You talk to him.
MRS. KELLY. You're the one that sees him.
SAL. Please don't start. Let's talk about this somewhere else!
MRS. KELLY. Start what?
SAL. *(Frustrated.)* What does Dad have to do with professional carpet cleaning?!
MRS. KELLY. *(No stopping her now.)* Because I don't need you to complain about the apartment. Okay? That is a whole separate topic. When we moved in there it was only supposed to be for a

few years. That was 1983. Do you understand? A marriage is a contractual agreement. Promises were made. Every injury has their equivalent. Do you know what the equivalent of injury is? Pain. Your father turned our house into a carnival of suffering. One day you'll understand the criminology behind it, behind his behavior. You don't marry someone and make promises, and then deny they ever existed. I worked two jobs so he could get his business started. I practically lost my hearing because of that job by the airport. I was teaching English as a second language to people who don't speak English, okay?! And there were constantly airplanes taking off. You try to conjugate verbs at LaGuardia. And I'm pregnant, getting home at ten or eleven o'clock at night. And he would say that this was all temporary. He needed a few years to get the business started, and then we'd move out of the city. Westchester, or New Jersey. He didn't want a child going to New York City schools. They're dangerous. It was okay for his wife to work in them, I guess. We were going to have a house, a backyard, insulation. Not the paper-thin walls you get in these apartments …

SAL. Mom, *please.* I can't take it anymore!!! *(Mr. Wells enters the waiting area, interrupting their argument. He's really wound up, but looks slightly better and more hopeful than the night before.)*

MR. WELLS. Oh good. Thanks for coming back …

SAL. How is he?

MR. WELLS. … My sister had to get back to her kids. And you were here in the beginning and I just felt like it was important for you to be here now.

MRS. KELLY. *(Understanding.)* Of course. How is he?

MR. WELLS. I know Lightfield knows you're here. I told him and I know he could hear me and it's important to him …

SAL. Good. Thank you.

MR. WELLS. … And where is the other one?

SAL. Josh?

MR. WELLS. Yeah. *(There's a pause. Sal does not know what to say.)*

SAL. *(Trying to sound positive.)* He'll be here. He's on his way right now. *(At that moment Adam enters the waiting area. Mr. Wells does not acknowledge him.)*

MR. WELLS. Okay, well, the good news is he's breathing on his own! He's no longer incubated …

ADAM. *(Correcting him.)* In*tub*ated. *(Mr. Wells turns towards Adam and glares at him.)*

MR. WELLS. *(Rudely.)* Excuse me?

ADAM. In*tub*ated.
MR. WELLS. *(Slightly irritated.)* Who are you?
ADAM. I'm Dr. Adam Levy, Josh's stepbrother.
MR. WELLS. Oh. Hm. Where is that kid?
ADAM. We don't know.
MR. WELLS. That sounds like him. What kind of doctor are you?
ADAM. Pediatric emergency medicine.
MR. WELLS. Well you're late. They had some trouble at first but then they brought in a toxicologist and got their act together.
ADAM. What's the prognosis?
MR. WELLS. *(Warming to him.)* They said it's still too early to say but potentially encouraging. His signs are coming back and his breathing's no longer assisted.
MRS. KELLY. Thank God. If there's anything you need us to do … *(Mr. Wells sits down for a moment to rest. He takes a deep breath.)*
MR. WELLS. I'm just glad you're back. It's a comfort to me. You know Lightfield's mother passed away a few years ago. She was an extraordinary woman, my wife. A jeweler. She made jewelry out of dichroic glass. That's where Lightfield got the artistic inclination. Definitely not from me. Anyway, she always said there were two ways of looking at things. Even our darkest moment could be considered a blessing. But ever since this all started here, I just can't see where the blessing would be. Where could there be a blessing in this? *(No one answers. No one knows what to say. Sorrowfully.)* You don't know what it's like. To look anguish in the eye. I've looked anguish in the eye before and I said please God don't let me look at it again. *(There is a silence. Mr. Wells turns to Sal.)* At some point later maybe you and I will sit down and you can help me understand what I've been missing.
SAL. Me?
MR. WELLS. Yes, you. And that other friend of yours. Where *is* he? Because I just don't understand. My son and I are close. We always have been. He talks to me. I always thought if he was going through something, he would come to me. So how do I explain this? I mean just last week we spent hours talking about everything in his life! School, friends, his career. We went to go see a poet he likes at the Y. Major Jackson. And then after we went out for burgers. On a Saturday night! My son was having a burger with me! So how do I explain this? *(Mr. Wells puts his head in his hands, overcome with grief.)*
SAL. Didn't Major Jackson write "Euphoria"?
MR. WELLS. *(Looking up.)* Yes, that was one of them. He did.

SAL. *(Matter-of-factly.)* It's a poem about getting high. *(Everyone looks at Sal. She realizes she probably just made a pretty big blunder.)* I mean, it's a poem about him discovering that he wants to be a poet, while he's getting high. *(There is an awkward silence. Everyone still looks at her. Sal can't dig herself out.)* I mean … I don't know what I mean. He also wrote a poem called "Blunts." *(There is an even more awkward silence.)*

MRS. KELLY. *(Apologetically.)* She's tired.

SAL. Yeah.

MRS. KELLY. She didn't sleep last night when we got home. I could hear her pacing around the apartment.

SAL. Yeah. I'm really sorry. *(Mr. Wells looks at her, defeated.)*

MR. WELLS. I'm going back upstairs. Come get me when Josh gets here … *(He starts to leave, and then stops again, still grappling with how this happened. Speaking almost more to himself than them.)* What is it with kids and drugs and violence and pressure? Where is it that we, as parents, go wrong? I look around and I don't know where the problem begins or ends. It's like a fuse that's been lit but you don't know who struck the match. And it burns and coils through homes and schools and neighborhoods, and at one point or another, every child is in its path. I've been watching with my eyes wide open. I'm not the only parent on a vigil. I try not to clock the hours that my son is out with his friends, but they're logged anyway on a watch that never stops ticking. And the kids blame the homes and the homes blame the schools and the schools blame the streets. And the streets, they don't blame no one. They're just there, watching us back. Full of goddamn secrets … *(He stops, and finally exits. Sal sits down and sulks. Mrs. Kelly looks at her and shakes her head. Adam sits down as well.)*

ADAM. He's right, you know. And it's especially worse after 9/11. The kids are more stressed out. Everybody is. Afraid of losing somebody. This is the city of the lost and the missing. *(No one speaks for a few beats.)*

SAL. *(To no one in particular.)* Lightfield wrote a poem about his mother dying. He said it felt like she disappeared from his life. Like a dream you can't remember when you wake up in the morning. *(They ignore her.)*

MRS. KELLY. *(To Adam, trying to make conversation.)* Are you married?

ADAM. Three years.

MRS. KELLY. Good for you. Wonderful. And what does she do?

ADAM. She's getting her Ph.D.

MRS. KELLY. Any kids?

ADAM. We're talking about it. We'll probably wait until my residency is over. Or she's out of school.

MRS. KELLY. Wonderful. That was the happiest moment of my life. When I had Sal.

SAL. *(Embarrassed.)* Mom, please!

MRS. KELLY. Of course it was. Nothing else compares.

ADAM. I'm sure. There's no way to understand it, until you've experienced it. To carry a baby to term. The bond is inextricable, like separating your own DNA. Right, Sal? *(To Mrs. Kelly.)* We were just talking about that. *(To Sal.)* What do you think?

SAL. I don't think.

ADAM. I'm sure you do.

MRS. KELLY. Don't be rude.

SAL. *(Casually, but pointedly.)* What do I think? Okay. I think some people spend their whole lives recovering from being born! *(Adam and Mrs. Kelly both stop and stare at Sal.)*

MRS. KELLY. Sal!

ADAM. Excuse me?

SAL. It makes sense, right? It's the best we ever have it, when you're a baby in the womb. Free food, free housing. You're as close to another human being as you'll ever be. Closer than love. The safety, the absolute, the everything in nothing. But then all of a sudden our time is up and we get pushed out of the birth canal and we don't have any idea what's on the other side, except that we're losing the only thing we know. And you realize that for some people, this is the most fundamental experience they've had, this loss, this fear of losing. And they spend their whole lives expecting it to happen again! People who are so lost in their own loss they can't differentiate between their failed marriage and — I don't know — carpet cleaner! *(There is a long, awkward pause. Mrs. Kelly is visibly embarrassed. No one really knows what to make of Sal. Adam finally breaks the silence. He clears his throat.)*

ADAM. You know, if you're interested, there are many good books on the cycles of life and death. From a biological standpoint. You can even go back farther than that and start with the five kingdoms, prokaryotes, protoctists, fungi, plants, and animals. *(Sal does not know what to make of this.)*

SAL. That is not what I meant.

ADAM. Oh. *(Mrs. Kelly glares at Sal and then gets up and exits.)*

SAL. *(To Adam.)* I think I'm talking more about psychology than biology.
ADAM. I understand.
SAL. *(Skeptically.)* Do you know anything about psychology?
ADAM. I'm a medical doctor.
SAL. So?
ADAM. Psychology is philosophy first, then science.
SAL. Okay, then.
ADAM. Nevertheless, I have been known to run in some mental health circles. *(Sal looks at him like he's crazy.)*
SAL. In the Bronx?
ADAM. It sounds like your situation is high-risk.
SAL. Meaning?
ADAM. You're experiencing the negative symptomatology of your mother's disorder. Eighty-two percent of Americans who meet the diagnostic criteria for depression never receive an official diagnosis.
SAL. If I translated that into English correctly, what are you talking about?
ADAM. What do you mean?
SAL. I'm not talking about *symptomalogy,* whatever that is, I'm just saying that my mother's let her whole life fall apart.
ADAM. So your mother's suffering from a bad attitude?
SAL. Yeah.
ADAM. And not an illness?
SAL. No.
ADAM. When did it start?
SAL. When they got divorced. *(Adam pauses.)*
ADAM. Oh. *(Thoughtful.)* Interesting. *(Beat.)* Who's afraid of losing who. You or her?
SAL. What?
ADAM. Were you ever separated from her when you younger?
SAL. Briefly.
ADAM. What do you mean?
SAL. I mean, when I was born. My grandma took care of me.
ADAM. For how long?
SAL. A month. I don't know. *(Becoming annoyed.)* What kind of "mental health circles" are you running in?
ADAM. Child developmental psychopathologists. It's just a hobby.
SAL. Oh.
ADAM. My wife's friends. *(Beat.)* There is a biochemical depressive disorder that affects some women after childbirth. It can be recur-

rent. In some clinically significant cases in which it does not easily remit, the infant needs to be separated from his or her mother until the situation is controlled. Then the child can be brought home. *(He pauses.)* Just a thought. *(Sal looks at him for a moment taking him in.)*
SAL. Psychopathology. It sounds … I don't know … violent.
ADAM. No. It's just studying the patterns of adaptation and maladaptation, the relations between biological, social, emotional, and cognitive responses. *(Suddenly the payphone begins to ring. Sal practically jumps out of her seat and lunges for the phone.)*
SAL. *(Hopefully.)* Hello? … Hello? … *(But no one is there. Dejected, she hangs it up. She turns to Adam, desperate to confide in somebody.)* Adam, if someone you knew was in a potentially dangerous situation … But you weren't sure. It's just a feeling. And that person isn't really the type you have to worry about. That he can protect himself. He's not really the type you have to worry about at all. But what would you do? Would you do something about it?
ADAM. Meaning?
SAL. Have you called your stepmother to see if she knows where Josh is?
ADAM. I tried a little while ago. I couldn't get through. *(Beat.)* Should I try again? *(Sal nods her head.)* I'll be right back. *(Adam takes his pager and his phone out and exits the waiting room. Sal sits with her head in her hands.)*
SAL. *(Desperate.)* Please, please help me. *(She waits. Mrs. Kelly enters excitedly [for her].)*
MRS. KELLY. *(Relieved, overjoyed.)* Did you hear the news?! He's okay! No permanent damage. He's talking with his father right now!
SAL. Really?!
MRS. KELLY. He pulled through! *(Sal looks at her, stunned. Happy. She starts to smile with joy and relief.)*
SAL. Can I go see him? *(Adam enters, interrupting the moment. They turn to him excitedly. Excited, relieved.)* Adam, did you hear the news?! It's Lightfield!
ADAM. *(Sensitively, but firmly.)* Sal, I think you might want to come with me. *(Beat.)* There are detectives over at the house. *(Blackout. Note: This blackout should be longer than the others.)*

Scene 2

Lights rise on the waiting room. The stage is empty. It is later, almost ten or eleven at night. The lights are dimmer now, and there is the glow of the vending machines in the corner. It is much quieter than before. We hear the faint sounds of the hospital in the background. A page for a doctor is heard offstage. It is low and muted, distant, from another room. The stage remains empty for some time. After a while, Mr. Wells enters the waiting room. He walks over to the vending machine and gets a soda, and then sits down. He is overtired and pensive. He waits. Shortly after, Mrs. Kelly enters the waiting room with a paper bag. She is wearing her coat.

MRS. KELLY. Sorry I took so long.
MR. WELLS. Not a problem. *(Mr. Wells sighs and shakes his head. Mrs. Kelly takes off her coat.)*
MRS. KELLY. I guess they close the cafeteria on Sunday nights.
MR. WELLS. Really?
MRS. KELLY. I found a deli that was open. I had to walk to Second Avenue.
MR. WELLS. The one on the corner was closed?
MRS. KELLY. Unfortunately.
MR. WELLS. Well, I'll throw out this soda then. I appreciate the cup of coffee. *(He goes to the garbage and throws his soda can in it. Mrs. Kelly takes out her cup of coffee and then hands him the bag.)*
MRS. KELLY. Here you go.
MR. WELLS. Thank you. *(He opens his coffee.)* Still no news?
MRS. KELLY. *(At a loss.)* Not a word … *(Mr. Wells takes a long sip.)* The homeless problem has gotten better in this city.
MR. WELLS. Sure has. *(They sit in silence for a few beats.)*
MRS. KELLY. Is Lightfield still sleeping?
MR. WELLS. He was.
MRS. KELLY. Good. *(A beat.)*
MR. WELLS. They woke him up for counseling.
MRS. KELLY. Oh.
MR. WELLS. Standard procedure.

MRS. KELLY. I understand.
MR. WELLS. A psychiatric evaluation was optional.
MRS. KELLY. That's … nice. *(They are silent again.)*
MR. WELLS. There's been nowhere to sit up there. My legs are really aching now.
MRS. KELLY. Couldn't a nurse have brought you a chair?
MR. WELLS. There's a thought. *(Mr. Wells shakes his head.)* Coffee's good. Better than what they have downstairs.
MRS. KELLY. That's true. The sandwiches weren't too bad.
MR. WELLS. No. Not too bad. And the hot meals.
MRS. KELLY. Yeah.
MR. WELLS. For lunch I had the veal marsala.
MRS. KELLY. Umm …
MR. WELLS. Not too bad.
MRS. KELLY. *(Lightly.)* A vacation from the everyday.
MR.WELLS. Sure. *(There is a pause.)*
MR. WELLS. I wonder what he's talking about up there.
MRS. KELLY. Lightfield?
MR. WELLS. Yeah. *(Pause, he feels the weight of this.)* My son. *(There is a tense silence. Mr. Wells darkens.)* I wonder what he's talking about.
MRS. KELLY. Hopefully he's doing some listening.
MR. WELLS. That's not like him.
MRS. KELLY. Oh. *(Mrs. Kelly doesn't respond, unsure of what to say. Mr. Wells thinks to himself for a little while, and then sharply puts down his coffee cup. He crumples the paper bag and tosses it on the floor.)*
MR. WELLS. Damnit! *(He lowers his head.)*
MRS. KELLY. Clifford? What is it? … *(Mr. Wells shakes his head sadly. He doesn't answer. Finally he looks up.)*
MR. WELLS. *(Slowly, sorrowfully.)* I feel a strong sense of … *culpability.*
MRS. KELLY. Excuse me?
MR. WELLS. *Culpability.* I have to acknowledge my role in this. I have to accept my answerability.
MRS. KELLY. There's no sense in blaming yourself.
MR. WELLS. There's no sense in *not* blaming myself! I'm his father. This is my fault too. Something *I* have done, or *not* done, drove him to this point. Some sense of hopelessness. Of not being understood.
MRS. KELLY. What do you mean?
MR. WELLS. He doesn't talk to me about *everything.* His shyness … What have I done wrong?
MRS. KELLY. *(Trying to find the right thing to say.)* Clifford …

MR. WELLS. He must feel lost. Like he can't trust me. Or relate to me. Sometimes I don't listen properly. I know he talked more to his mother. It's not my fault she's gone. She was an extraordinary woman. She made jewelry out of dichroic glass.

MRS. KELLY. I understand. *(Mrs. Kelly sits next to him hopelessly.)*

MR. WELLS. It's a process. A way of treating the glass that allows color to come through. This is my fault … *(Mr. Wells wipes his eyes.)*

MRS. KELLY. Clifford. Don't be upset. He's going to be alright …

MR. WELLS. Well, it must be easy for you to say. Your daughter works hard in school. She hasn't gotten in this type of trouble. She's smart. Polite. She's keeping it together. And she's nothing like Josh — the crazy one! Disappearing like this — in thin air! *(Mrs. Kelly shakes her head sadly.)*

MRS. KELLY. *(Sorrowfully.)* I wish it were that simple. *(A beat.)* But it never is, is it?

MR. WELLS. No. *(A deep, anguished sigh.)* I guess it never is. *(They sit in silence. They are interrupted when Sal enters the waiting room wearing her jacket. She walks over to the chairs and takes a seat away from Mrs. Kelly and Mr. Wells. She stares blankly ahead of her. They both look at her, unsure of what to say. There is an awkward pause. Searching.)* Sal. Good. Any news? *(Sal doesn't say anything. She seems disoriented, exhausted. Mr. Wells rises to his feet.)* Well, I better get back. I'll go see if he's finished now. *(He exits. There is a tense silence. Mrs. Kelly looks at Sal, concerned, waiting for some answers.)*

SAL. You're still here …

MRS. KELLY. It's late.

SAL. What time is it?

MRS. KELLY. Almost eleven. *(Sal takes off her jacket and holds it close to her.)* I spoke to your father. He said you'll stay with him starting tomorrow. *(Sal doesn't respond. She glances uneasily at her watch and the pay phone.)* You were gone a long time. *(Sal stands up and goes to the wall near the pay phone and paces. She is agitated, nervous.)* Do you want to talk about it?

SAL. *(Defensively.)* It's not my fault.

MRS. KELLY. What's not?

SAL. *(Reluctantly.)* I got lost.

MRS. KELLY. When?

SAL. When I left Josh's house.

MRS. KELLY. How?

SAL. *(Disoriented, full of adrenaline and confusion and fear.)* … I was going to take the C at 103rd and then get the crosstown. So I walked out of their building and I went to their corner, and the cars seemed to be going uptown, so I assumed it was Amsterdam and I just kept walking. I didn't look at the sign. But then all of a sudden I couldn't remember which way his street went. I didn't know which way I was heading. Was I walking towards Broadway or Columbus? And then, I don't know what happened, suddenly everything started to look unfamiliar. There was a supermarket at the next corner that I'd never seen before. A big Pathmark. And people were coming in and out. And I thought about asking someone for directions but then nobody in that neighborhood ever really looks like they know where they're going either. So I kept going up the street and I remember knowing that I should have passed Broadway by then. And when I crossed the street, I could see the moon reflecting off the water through the trees across the street, and I realized I had walked all the way to Riverside. But the weird thing was, I didn't turn around. I walked up to somebody's front steps instead and sat down because I felt too tired to go back. Really lethargic, like I just couldn't take another step. So I sat there for a while, and I could see someone watching television through a window across the street and I just kept staring. Staring at how beautiful it was, the way the television looked in the dark, the way the light kept moving. And after a while, I don't know how long, a woman walked up to the building with her dog and started talking to me. She said there'd been an accident a few blocks down with tons of police, and that if I was going to be walking around I should be careful. That there had been a bad accident and that whenever there's an emergency, the streets are a little worse in the surrounding areas because all the criminals feel like temporarily the heat is off. Like the cops are busy on 97th Street so I don't have to worry if I just rob someone at gunpoint on 105th, like a built-in diversionary tactic, that sort of thing. But it took this woman about twenty minutes to tell me all this, because half of her conversation was directed at me and half at her dog. As if he was going to contribute to the conversation. So finally I got up and left. I took another street and went to the subway. And all that time I'd been walking around, I never heard any sirens … *(Sal stops, she looks at her mother.)*

MRS. KELLY. You lost track of time.

SAL. Yeah.

MRS. KELLY. Are you hungry? I'll get you something to eat.

SAL. No. But I'll sit here. I'm too tired to eat anything. *(Sal sits, at the opposite end of the room from her mother.)*

MRS. KELLY. Are they going to call you, if there's news?
SAL. Here?
MRS. KELLY. Yeah.
SAL. *(Gesturing to the pay phone.)* I gave them this number. But there probably won't be news tonight.
MRS. KELLY. Were you helpful?
SAL. Yes.
MRS. KELLY. What did you tell them?
SAL. I told them what I know.
MRS. KELLY. Which is?
SAL. They were going to meet someone to buy a gun in the park. The problem was over this kid Frank Sanchez. I told them everything right when I got there.
MRS. KELLY. Who?
SAL. The two detectives, Josh's mom and his stepfather.
MRS. KELLY. But you were helpful?
SAL. Yes. They knew most of it, I mean, there's a rumor going around, about what happened. They knew that the kid there was the trouble over, Frank Sanchez, turned out to be in the same gang as the kid they were going to buy the gun from. So Farland must have found this out, because apparently he never went. Maybe he tried to call Josh to tell him not to go. And Josh just didn't get the page or the message. Maybe he was on the subway. So he showed up anyway, he showed up in Farland's place. And he was set up. *(Sal stops. Her face has lost all its color.)* I feel strange. Like I can't feel my feet.
MRS. KELLY. You're tired.
SAL. I feel like I'm underwater.
MRS. KELLY. Do you want something to drink? *(Sal nods. Mrs. Kelly goes to the vending machine. She puts in some quarters and gets Sal a soda.)* So the detectives won't need to ask you any more questions?
SAL. Not right now. They were fine. All business. One of them actually said his nephew goes to my school.
MRS. KELLY. How about his parents?
SAL. Josh's parents? Or, I mean, his mom and his stepfather, Dr. Levy? He's even worse than Adam.
MRS. KELLY. How do you mean?
SAL. I couldn't understand a word he said!
MRS. KELLY. Oh.
SAL. He kept talking about something called "street ethnography," and asking the detectives what "data" they had. And hadn't the juvenile division of the NYPD done anything? … And couldn't this have

been prevented? … He referred to Josh and his friends as "at-risk samples"! *(Sal takes a sip of her soda.)* And his mom. She was worse, the absolute worst. She was totally out to lunch. She offered the detectives coffee but then didn't actually know how to use the coffeemaker. It being the middle of the night and the person that normally operates the machinery, their housekeeper, is at home in Queens! So finally I couldn't take it anymore. I needed to get away from the insanity. So I went into Josh's room and sat on his bed for a while. I looked at all the trophies he has in his window from his chess tournaments, and I sat in there and waited. But it felt really strange. The room was very neat. The bed hadn't been slept in. And there was a history handout on his desk that we had done almost two weeks ago when we were doing Reconstruction. And the teacher had made this whole point about when the President vetoed the Wade-Davis Bill, it was considered the opening shot between him and the Congressional Radicals. And that's all Josh had written on his handout, "The opening shot." So I sat in there for a while and I knew something was wrong. And when I went back into the living room, do you know what I found out? Josh had been kicked out of the house over a week ago. He hadn't been home in over a week. *(Sal begins to cry.)* So this whole mess might not have happened, if he could have just gone home! But it's too late now. So I left. I couldn't take it anymore. They said they'll call when there's news. And I could still overhear them when I was leaving. When I was in the hallway waiting for the elevator and I could still hear their voices … talking about a search in Central Park and the surrounding areas … So I'll just wait, that's all … And I'm sure everything will turn out okay. Don't you think? *(Sal stops, exhausted. She looks at her mother, who is at a loss for words. She slowly leans her head back against the chair and briefly closes her eyes. They sit in silence. Sal lifts her head. Quietly:)* His mother said she just couldn't stand it anymore. She said sometimes he was gone for days. *(Sal pauses. She looks at her mother.)* What do you do when you wait for me?

MRS. KELLY. I read. Watch television, sometimes. Look at the photo album. *(Gently, as if a lullaby.)* I like to sit there and look at the pictures and dream about you. When you were a baby. And they brought you back home to me. We weren't separated anymore. We were a family again. And the whole world was new. *(Blackout.)*

Scene 3

Lights rise to dim on the waiting room. It is just a few moments later. Mrs. Kelly sits quietly. Sal lies across a few chairs, asleep. She uses her jacket as a pillow. Suddenly we hear the sound of Mr. Wells' voice from offstage.

MR. WELLS. *(From offstage.)* Sal … Catharine? *(He peaks his head into the waiting area.)* Oh good! I just wanted to tell you he's ready to go! They're bringing him downstairs right now. *(Mr. Wells exits hurriedly. Sal rises sleepily as Mrs. Kelly gathers her belongings. They put on their jackets, and walk towards the door. They are finally leaving the hospital. They exit. The room is now empty, deserted. It is silent except for the hum of the vending machines. A crumpled paper bag remains on the floor. After a few moments, the pay phone begins to ring, abruptly, piercing the silence. It rings continuously. Sal reenters the waiting room and stares at the phone, unsure of what to do. Mrs. Kelly stands in the entrance behind her. Sal walks over and picks it up.)*
SAL. *(Into the phone, her voice weak.)* Hello? … Un-huh … This is … Un-huh … I see … Okay … Okay. *(Sal slowly puts the phone down. She turns towards her mother, devastated, but hopeful. Mrs. Kelly looks at her. With something closer than love. From offstage we hear Mr. Wells.)*
MR. WELLS. *(From offstage.)* Sal … Catherine … He's coming…!
SAL. They found him. *(Mrs. Kelly opens her arms. Sal goes to them. Blackout.)*

End of Play

PROPERTY LIST

Pager (JOSHUA)
Cigarettes, lighter (JOSHUA)
Car keys, change (SAL)
Six-pack of Budweiser, backpack (JOSHUA)
Large jar of peanut butter (JOSHUA)
Mirror, lipstick, backpack (SAL)
Quarter (JOSHUA)
Soda (SAL, MR. WELLS, MRS. KELLY)
Plastic container with sandwich (MRS. KELLY)
Pager, cell phone (ADAM)
Paper bag with two cups of coffee (MRS. KELLY)

SOUND EFFECTS

Pager
Page for a doctor over a loudspeaker
Footsteps
Phone ring
Ambulances

NEW PLAYS

★ **MONTHS ON END by Craig Pospisil.** In comic scenes, one for each month of the year, we follow the intertwined worlds of a circle of friends and family whose lives are poised between happiness and heartbreak. "…a triumph…these twelve vignettes all form crucial pieces in the eternal puzzle known as human relationships, an area in which the playwright displays an assured knowledge that spans deep sorrow to unbounded happiness." *–Ann Arbor News.* "…rings with emotional truth, humor…[an] endearing contemplation on love…entertaining and satisfying." *–Oakland Press.* [5M, 5W] ISBN: 0-8222-1892-5

★ **GOOD THING by Jessica Goldberg.** Brings us into the households of John and Nancy Roy, forty-something high-school guidance counselors whose marriage has been increasingly on the rocks and Dean and Mary, recent graduates struggling to make their way in life. "…a blend of gritty social drama, poetic humor and unsubtle existential contemplation…" *–Variety.* [3M, 3W] ISBN: 0-8222-1869-0

★ **THE DEAD EYE BOY by Angus MacLachlan.** Having fallen in love at their Narcotics Anonymous meeting, Billy and Shirley-Diane are striving to overcome the past together. But their relationship is complicated by the presence of Sorin, Shirley-Diane's fourteen-year-old son, a damaged reminder of her dark past. "…a grim, insightful portrait of an unmoored family…" *–NY Times.* "MacLachlan's play isn't for the squeamish, but then, tragic stories delivered at such an unrelenting fever pitch rarely are." *–Variety.* [1M, 1W, 1 boy] ISBN: 0-8222-1844-5

★ **[SIC] by Melissa James Gibson.** In adjacent apartments three young, ambitious neighbors come together to discuss, flirt, argue, share their dreams and plan their futures with unequal degrees of deep hopefulness and abject despair. "A work…concerned with the sound and power of language…" *–NY Times.* "…a wonderfully original take on urban friendship and the comedy of manners—a *Design for Living* for our times…" *–NY Observer.* [3M, 2W] ISBN: 0-8222-1872-0

★ **LOOKING FOR NORMAL by Jane Anderson.** Roy and Irma's twenty-five-year marriage is thrown into turmoil when Roy confesses that he is actually a woman trapped in a man's body, forcing the couple to wrestle with the meaning of their marriage and the delicate dynamics of family. "Jane Anderson's bittersweet transgender domestic comedy-drama …is thoughtful and touching and full of wit and wisdom. A real audience pleaser." *–Hollywood Reporter.* [5M, 4W] ISBN: 0-8222-1857-7

★ **ENDPAPERS by Thomas McCormack.** The regal Joshua Maynard, the old and ailing head of a mid-sized, family-owned book-publishing house in New York City, must name a successor. One faction in the house backs a smart, "pragmatic" manager, the other faction a smart, "sensitive" editor and both factions fear what the other's man could do to this house—and to them. "If Kaufman and Hart had undertaken a comedy about the publishing business, they might have written *Endpapers*…a breathlessly fast, funny, and thoughtful comedy …keeps you amused, guessing, and often surprised…profound in its empathy for the paradoxes of human nature." *–NY Magazine.* [7M, 4W] ISBN: 0-8222-1908-5

★ **THE PAVILION by Craig Wright.** By turns poetic and comic, romantic and philosophical, this play asks old lovers to face the consequences of difficult choices made long ago. "The script's greatest strength lies in the genuineness of its feeling." *–Houston Chronicle.* "Wright's perceptive, gently witty writing makes this familiar situation fresh and thoroughly involving." *–Philadelphia Inquirer.* [2M, 1W (flexible casting)] ISBN: 0-8222-1898-4

NEW PLAYS

★ **BE AGGRESSIVE by Annie Weisman.** Vista Del Sol is paradise, sandy beaches, avocado-lined streets. But for seventeen-year-old cheerleader Laura, everything changes when her mother is killed in a car crash, and she embarks on a journey to the Spirit Institute of the South where she can learn "cheer" with Bible belt intensity. "…filled with lingual gymnastics…stylized rapid-fire dialogue…" *–Variety*. "…a new, exciting, and unique voice in the American theatre…" *–BackStage West*. [1M, 4W, extras] ISBN: 0-8222-1894-1

★ **FOUR by Christopher Shinn.** Four people struggle desperately to connect in this quiet, sophisticated, moving drama. "…smart, broken-hearted…Mr. Shinn has a precocious and forgiving sense of how power shifts in the game of sexual pursuit…He promises to be a playwright to reckon with…" *–NY Times*. "A voice emerges from an American place. It's got humor, sadness and a fresh and touching rhythm that tell of the loneliness and secrets of life…[a] poetic, haunting play." *–NY Post*. [3M, 1W] ISBN: 0-8222-1850-X

★ **WONDER OF THE WORLD by David Lindsay-Abaire.** A madcap picaresque involving Niagara Falls, a lonely tour-boat captain, a pair of bickering private detectives and a husband's dirty little secret. "Exceedingly whimsical and playfully wicked. Winning and genial. A top-drawer production." *–NY Times*. "Full frontal lunacy is on display. A most assuredly fresh and hilarious tragicomedy of marital discord run amok…absolutely hysterical…" *–Variety*. [3M, 4W (doubling)] ISBN: 0-8222-1863-1

★ **QED by Peter Parnell.** Nobel Prize-winning physicist and all-around genius Richard Feynman holds forth with captivating wit and wisdom in this fascinating biographical play that originally starred Alan Alda. "QED is a seductive mix of science, human affections, moral courage, and comic eccentricity. It reflects on, among other things, death, the absence of God, travel to an unexplored country, the pleasures of drumming, and the need to know and understand." *–NY Magazine*. "Its rhythms correspond to the way that people—even geniuses—approach and avoid highly emotional issues, and it portrays Feynman with affection and awe." *–The New Yorker*. [1M, 1W] ISBN: 0-8222-1924-7

★ **UNWRAP YOUR CANDY by Doug Wright.** Alternately chilling and hilarious, this deliciously macabre collection of four bedtime tales for adults is guaranteed to keep you awake for nights on end. "Engaging and intellectually satisfying…a treat to watch." *–NY Times*. "Fiendishly clever. Mordantly funny and chilling. Doug Wright teases, freezes and zaps us." *–Village Voice*. "Four bite-size plays that bite back." *–Variety*. [flexible casting] ISBN: 0-8222-1871-2

★ **FURTHER THAN THE FURTHEST THING by Zinnie Harris.** On a remote island in the middle of the Atlantic secrets are buried. When the outside world comes calling, the islanders find their world blown apart from the inside as well as beyond. "Harris winningly produces an intimate and poetic, as well as political, family saga." *–Independent (London)*. "Harris' enthralling adventure of a play marks a departure from stale, well-furrowed theatrical terrain." *–Evening Standard (London)*. [3M, 2W] ISBN: 0-8222-1874-7

★ **THE DESIGNATED MOURNER by Wallace Shawn.** The story of three people living in a country where what sort of books people like to read and how they choose to amuse themselves becomes both firmly personal and unexpectedly entangled with questions of survival. "This is a playwright who does not just tell you what it is like to be arrested at night by goons or to fall morally apart and become an aimless yet weirdly contented ghost yourself. He has the originality to make you feel it." *–Times (London)*. "A fascinating play with beautiful passages of writing…" *–Variety*. [2M, 1W] ISBN: 0-8222-1848-8

NEW PLAYS

★ **SHEL'S SHORTS by Shel Silverstein.** Lauded poet, songwriter and author of children's books, the incomparable Shel Silverstein's short plays are deeply infused with the same wicked sense of humor that made him famous. "…[a] childlike honesty and twisted sense of humor." *–Boston Herald.* "…terse dialogue and an absurdity laced with a tang of dread give [*Shel's Shorts*] more than a trace of Samuel Beckett's comic existentialism." *–Boston Phoenix.* [flexible casting] ISBN: 0-8222-1897-6

★ **AN ADULT EVENING OF SHEL SILVERSTEIN by Shel Silverstein.** Welcome to the darkly comic world of Shel Silverstein, a world where nothing is as it seems and where the most innocent conversation can turn menacing in an instant. These ten imaginative plays vary widely in content, but the style is unmistakable. "…[*An Adult Evening*] shows off Silverstein's virtuosic gift for wordplay…[and] sends the audience out…with a clear appreciation of human nature as perverse and laughable." *–NY Times.* [flexible casting] ISBN: 0-8222-1873-9

★ **WHERE'S MY MONEY? by John Patrick Shanley.** A caustic and sardonic vivisection of the institution of marriage, laced with the author's inimitable razor-sharp wit. "…Shanley's gift for acid-laced one-liners and emotionally tumescent exchanges is certainly potent…" *–Variety.* "…lively, smart, occasionally scary and rich in reverse wisdom." *–NY Times.* [3M, 3W] ISBN: 0-8222-1865-8

★ **A FEW STOUT INDIVIDUALS by John Guare.** A wonderfully screwy comedy-drama that figures Ulysses S. Grant in the throes of writing his memoirs, surrounded by a cast of fantastical characters, including the Emperor and Empress of Japan, the opera star Adelina Patti and Mark Twain. "Guare's smarts, passion and creativity skyrocket to awesome heights…" *–Star Ledger.* "…precisely the kind of good new play that you might call an everyday miracle…every minute of it is fresh and newly alive…" *–Village Voice.* [10M, 3W] ISBN: 0-8222-1907-7

★ **BREATH, BOOM by Kia Corthron.** A look at fourteen years in the life of Prix, a Bronx native, from her ruthless girl-gang leadership at sixteen through her coming to maturity at thirty. "…vivid world, believable and eye-opening, a place worthy of a dramatic visit, where no one would want to live but many have to." *–NY Times.* "…rich with humor, terse vernacular strength and gritty detail…" *–Variety.* [1M, 9W] ISBN: 0-8222-1849-6

★ **THE LATE HENRY MOSS by Sam Shepard.** Two antagonistic brothers, Ray and Earl, are brought together after their father, Henry Moss, is found dead in his seedy New Mexico home in this classic Shepard tale. "…His singular gift has been for building mysteries out of the ordinary ingredients of American family life…" *–NY Times.* "…rich moments …Shepard finds gold." *–LA Times.* [7M, 1W] ISBN: 0-8222-1858-5

★ **THE CARPETBAGGER'S CHILDREN by Horton Foote.** One family's history spanning from the Civil War to WWII is recounted by three sisters in evocative, intertwining monologues. "…bittersweet music—[a] rhapsody of ambivalence…in its modest, garrulous way…theatrically daring." *–The New Yorker.* [3W] ISBN: 0-8222-1843-7

★ **THE NINA VARIATIONS by Steven Dietz.** In this funny, fierce and heartbreaking homage to *The Seagull*, Dietz puts Chekhov's star-crossed lovers in a room and doesn't let them out. "A perfect little jewel of a play…" *–Shepherdstown Chronicle.* "…a delightful revelation of a writer at play; and also an odd, haunting, moving theater piece of lingering beauty." *–Eastside Journal (Seattle).* [1M, 1W (flexible casting)] ISBN: 0-8222-1891-7